CLASSIC STORYBOOK

COLLECTION

This book belongs to:

_____

This edition published by Parragon Books Ltd in 2014

Parragon Books Ltd
Chartist House
15–17 Trim Street
Bath BA1 1HA, UK
www.parragon.com

ISBN 978-1-4723-5508-9
Printed in China

Bath · New York · Cologne · Melbourne · Delhi
Hong Kong · Shenzhen · Singapore · Amsterdam

It was another busy day for the fairies of Pixie Hollow. A fairy named Zarina was strolling towards the Pixie Dust Depot where she worked. As fairies use pixie dust to fly the other fairies assumed Zarina was walking because she had run out of pixie dust, which was surprising, since she was a dust-keeper fairy!

All of Pixie Hollow relied on the pixie dust that Zarina packaged at the Depot. She was completely fascinated by pixie dust. She had just sprinkled some on her hair to see what it would do, when the head dust-keeper, Fairy Gary, appeared. Today, it was Zarina's turn for Blue Dust Duty.

As Zarina followed Fairy Gary to the Blue Pixie Dust vault, she peppered him with questions. She wanted to know if they could make other colours of pixie dust.

Fairy Gary warned her, "Dust-keepers are forbidden to tamper with pixie dust." As she transferred some of it to a small bottle Gary also reminded her that she was not allowed to touch the Blue Dust directly.

When the bottle was ready, Zarina and Fairy Gary
flew up to the boughs of the Pixie Dust Tree. Fairy Gary
poured the Blue Dust into the special container at the top.
Instantly, the amount of golden dust the tree produced
flowed faster and grew brighter.

"Takes the golden dust from a trickle to a roar,"
Fairy Gary explained.

Later, back at her cottage where she had been secretly saving up her pixie dust, Zarina found a speck of Blue Dust in her hair. She was inspired to try again one of her many failed pixie-dust experiments, this time adding a tiny bit of the Blue Dust. Suddenly, the dust turned orange and a smile lit up her face.

Zarina couldn't wait to show Tinker Bell her discovery. She brought Tink to her cottage. She showed Tink how to make the orange dust let her bend moonbeams.

"I'm doing more!" declared Zarina. And she put Tink to work stirring while various pots of dust began to explode around them. Soon they had purple dust that let Zarina create a fast-flying whirlwind.

To make pink dust, Zarina had used two slivers of the Blue Dust.

"Zarina, I really think you should stop!" Tink said firmly.

Surprised by Tink's reaction, Zarina bumped into a table and spilled all of the pink dust onto a nearby plant.

Suddenly, thick vines sprouted from the plant and tore through the cottage.

The vines twisted and turned, spreading across Pixie Hollow and destroying everything in their path – including the Dust Depot!

Queen Clarion wanted to know what had happened, and as soon as Fairy Gary saw the pink dust, he knew it was Zarina. She tried to apologize, but he interrupted to tell her she could no longer be a dust-keeper.

Zarina was devastated. She rushed back home, packed her things and left Pixie Hollow.

A year passed without a word from Zarina and it was time for the annual Four Seasons Festival. Every talent from every season would be on display!

Everyone was enchanted as the winter fairies gave a spectacular show on the ice.

Tink was still hard at work, fiddling with the
latch on an elaborate music box.

She looked up as the winter fairies skated by.
"That's my sister!" said Tink proudly
as Periwinkle frosted flowers in front of
the crowd.

While everyone was watching the show, Tink and her friends spotted Zarina emerging from the shadows. She sprinkled pink dust behind the crowd. Soon, big, red poppies began to sprout around the ampitheatre.

Rosetta knew the pollen from the flowers would put everyone to sleep. "Guys! We gotta hide! Now!" she cried.

As the fairies hid backstage, Zarina flew to the dust vault to steal the Blue Pixie Dust.

Clank had missed the beginning of the show, so when he returned to the ampitheatre, he was shocked to find that every last fairy was asleep. Then he heard cries for help from backstage. Tink and her pals were trapped inside the music box!

After Clank had freed them, the fairies
looked at the snoozing audience. Clank told
Tink that he had seen Zarina flying towards
the Dust Depot.

The fairies discovered that Zarina had stolen all of the Blue Pixie Dust.

"Why would Zarina do this?" asked Vidia.

The fairies knew they had no choice but to find Zarina. Their supply of golden pixie dust depended on that Blue Dust!

Tink asked Clank to take care of all the sleeping fairies, then set off with her friends to find Zarina before it was too late for Pixie Hollow!

The fairies zoomed through the woods after Zarina.

As they struggled to catch up, a heavy fog rolled in. Silvermist explained that they were nearing the coast.

The fairies flew higher and spotted a pirate ship off in the distance!

"They must have captured her and forced her to take the dust," said Tink.

Sure enough, a small rowing boat carrying three pirates was making its way towards the ship.

The fairies looked in and saw a blue glow!

Inside the boat, Zarina was holding up the Blue Pixie Dust triumphantly.

"Let me just say your plan worked perfectly ... Captain," said James, the cabin boy.

The other pirates, Port and Starboard, bowed to their tiny leader.

The fairies couldn't believe it – Zarina was now a pirate!

"Let's just get the dust and get out of here," ordered Tink.

The fairies sprang into action. Rosetta grew seaweed that held the oars in place. Iridessa reflected a moonbeam into James's eyes, making it hard for him to see. Silvermist rocked the boat with a wave. Finally, Vidia snatched the Blue Dust and tossed it to Tink.

The fairies headed for the shore, but Zarina
soon caught up with them and demanded that
they return the dust. Tink refused. "This dust
belongs to Pixie Hollow," she said.

Zarina responded by hurling a fistful of
multicoloured pixie dust at the fairies.

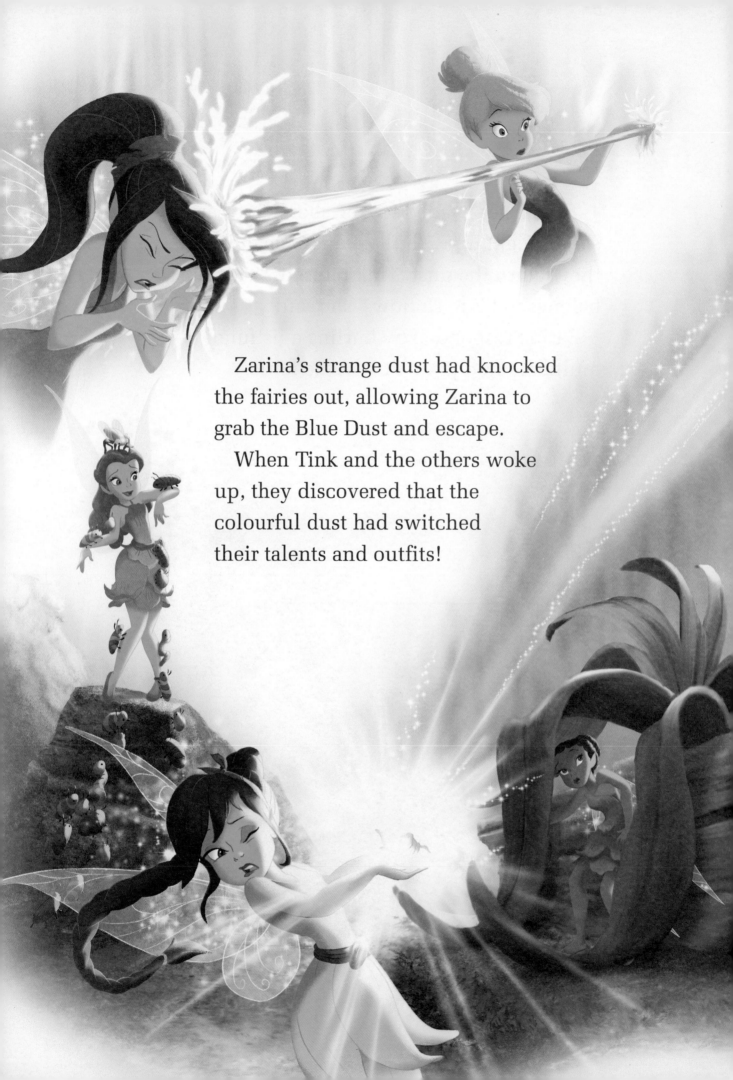

Zarina's strange dust had knocked
the fairies out, allowing Zarina to
grab the Blue Dust and escape.

When Tink and the others woke
up, they discovered that the
colourful dust had switched
their talents and outfits!

Tink was now a water fairy! She tried to part a nearby waterfall, but Silvermist, now a fast-flying fairy, bumped Tink as she passed by. Tink lost control over the water, which then pushed the fairies down a long, winding, leaf.

The friends rode the leaf down to a beach, where Rosetta landed on a crocodile egg. The egg started to crack and a baby croc hatched from it. He hugged Rosetta tightly. Rosetta was startled – she wasn't used to her new animal talent!

"It's okay! They become attached to the first thing they see," Fawn reassured her.

Tinker Bell suddenly noticed that the pirate ship was gone. The fairies could not fly because their wings were wet so Vidia, who was now a tinker fairy, took charge. She made a boat out of the croc egg. The fairies climbed in and Silvermist pulled them along the water.

Then a giant wave carried them straight to the ship!

The fairies landed inside one of the cannons. "Twenty-one gun salute to the captain!" announced a pirate named Yang.

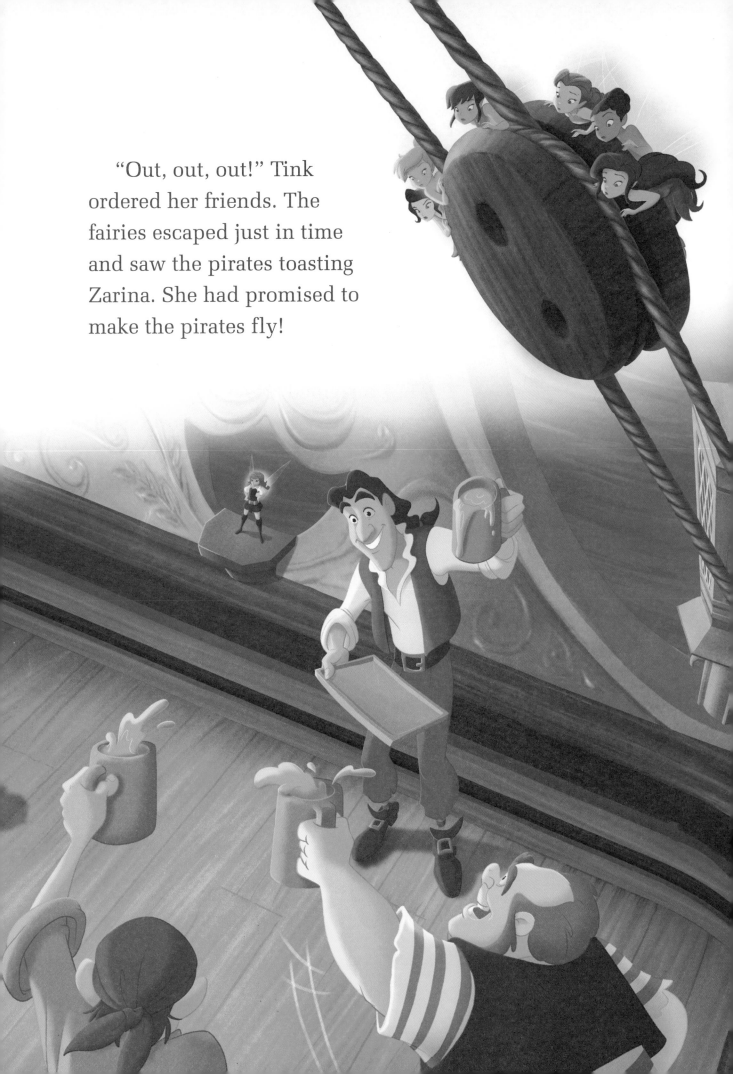

"Out, out, out!" Tink ordered her friends. The fairies escaped just in time and saw the pirates toasting Zarina. She had promised to make the pirates fly!

The pirate crew couldn't wait.
They imagined travelling the skies
beyond the second star, dropping down
on the Mainland wherever they pleased.
It was going to be so easy to steal lots of
treasure. After all, no one would be able
to catch a pirate that flew!

Tink and the other fairies flew up to the crow's nest. Suddenly, they were gripped by fear. The pirate ship was sailing straight for the dreaded Skull Rock! The dark and scary cave was the last place they wanted to go!

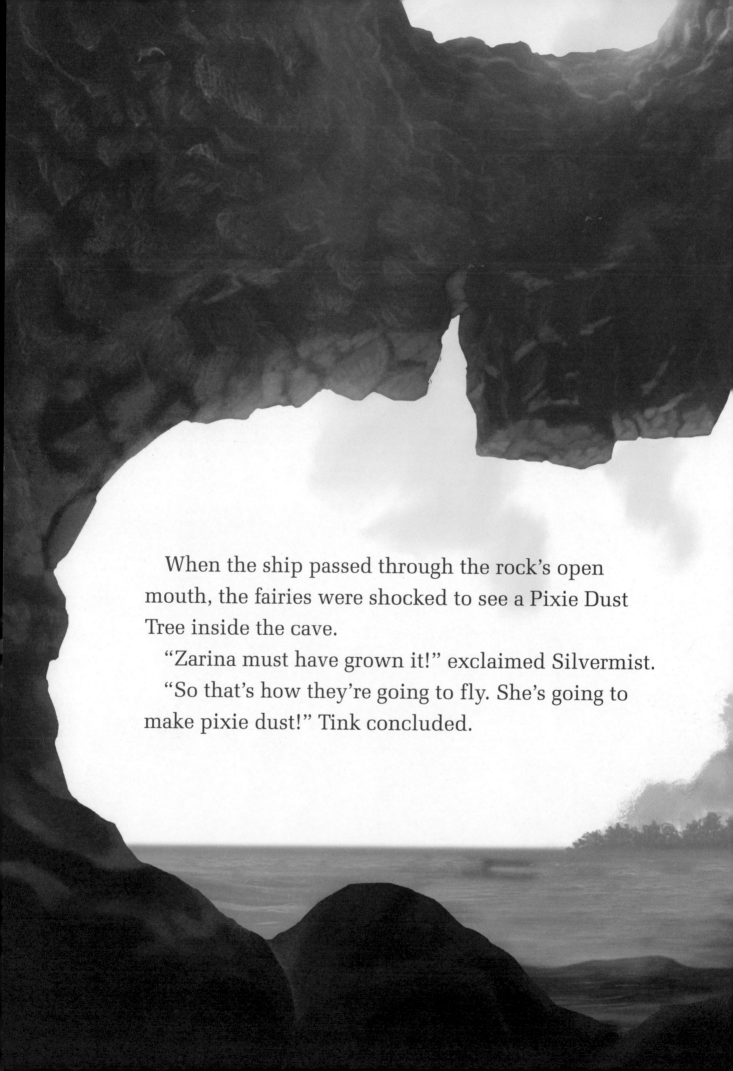

When the ship passed through the rock's open
mouth, the fairies were shocked to see a Pixie Dust
Tree inside the cave.

"Zarina must have grown it!" exclaimed Silvermist.

"So that's how they're going to fly. She's going to
make pixie dust!" Tink concluded.

The ship docked inside the cave. Zarina went to her cabin where James had brought her some food. Tink, Vidia and Silvermist slipped in behind him, while the others listened through the door.

James watched Zarina preparing the Blue Pixie Dust. "So the secret is to put the Blue Dust directly into the tree. Very impressive, Captain!" he said.

Zarina jingled as she poured the Blue Dust into a bottle. James was the only pirate who could understand fairy language, for he had become her most trusted friend.

The fairies joined back up with Rosetta, Iridessa and Fawn and quickly followed Zarina to the Pixie Dust Tree. Unfortunately, Iridessa – now a garden fairy – accidentally touched a branch which made it grow so violently that it pushed them out of their hiding place and straight into Zarina!

Zarina whistled and the pirates swooped in.
They captured Tink and the other fairies in a net.
"Don't do this," pleaded Tinker Bell. "Come
back home. You don't belong here."

Zarina refused. "This is exactly where
I belong," she declared.

"We appreciate what she can do,"
James chimed in. "Treasure it, actually."

Zarina ordered the ship's cook to take
the fairies away. He put them in a crab cage in
his galley and locked it tight.

"Welcome to your new cabin," he said.

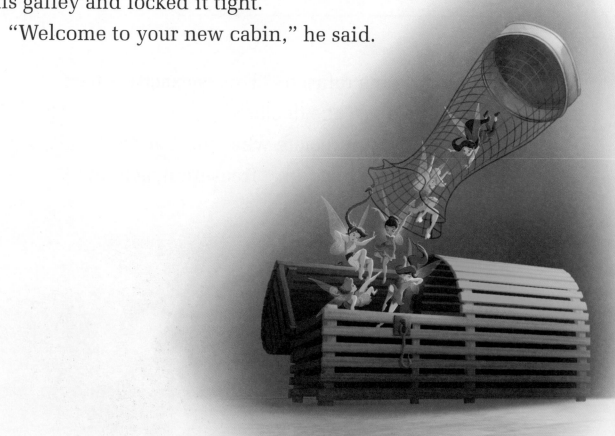

Meanwhile, Zarina added Blue Pixie Dust to the
Pixie Dust Tree. Everyone held their breath and waited.
The tree glowed and shook, and then ... produced a
tiny bit of golden pixie dust!

"We're going to fly!" James cried. Zarina beamed at
him with happiness.

In the galley of the ship, Tink and her friends had lifted their crab-cage prison off the ground and stuck their legs between the slats so they could run away.

But the cook stopped them from escaping
by putting the crate on a table and weighing it
down with a sack of potatoes.

Meanwhile the pirates were celebrating outside at the Pixie Dust Tree. The golden pixie dust was flowing from it steadily! Zarina sprinkled some on James and taught him how to fly.

"As long as we have the Blue Dust, we'll never run out of pixie dust, right Zarina?" he asked.

"Yes," Zarina jingled back.

"Well, then, we won't need you anymore," James
announced! He grabbed the stunned Zarina and locked her
inside a lantern!

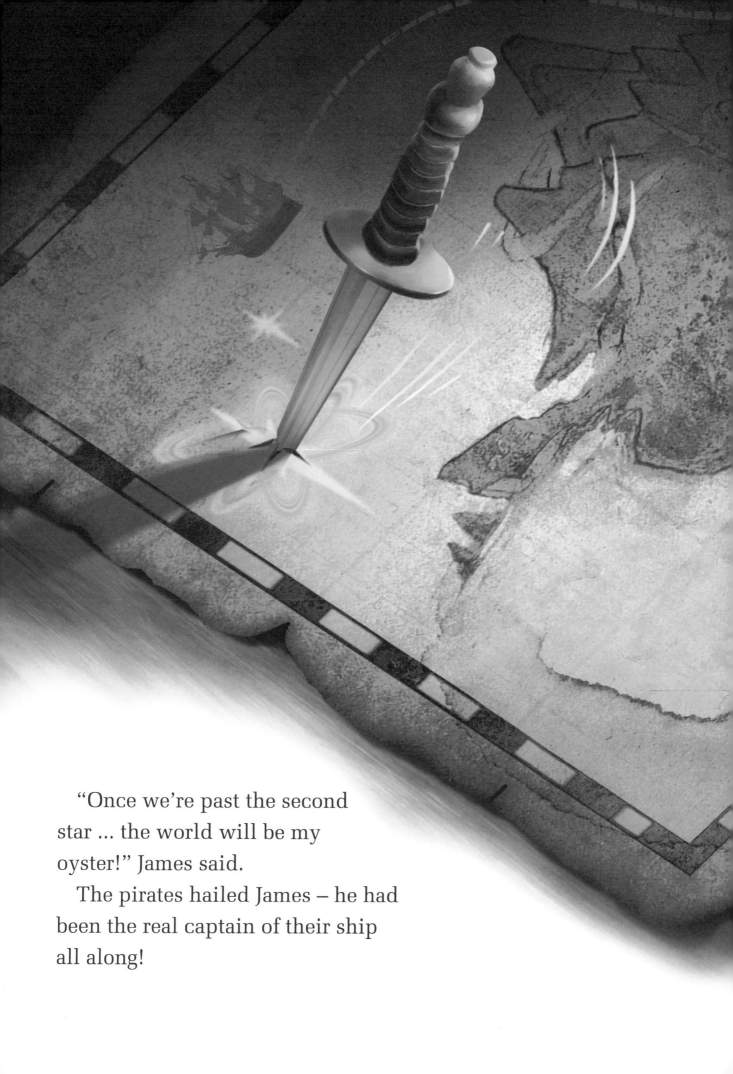

"Once we're past the second star ... the world will be my oyster!" James said.

The pirates hailed James – he had been the real captain of their ship all along!

Down in the galley, Rosetta's crocodile had
hopped through a cannon hole. The baby croc
pulled down the crate holding the fairies.
He wanted his favourite fairy friend!

The cook tried to catch his prisoners, but the croc
bit him! The fairies didn't have to worry about
the cook anymore!

The fairies snuck off the ship and snatched the bottle of Blue Dust from the Pixie Dust Tree.

"Return that Blue Dust!" James called to the fairies as they flew across the deck. He dangled the lantern holding Zarina above the water. "Or your friend is done for!"

The fairies didn't want Zarina to get hurt. Tink sadly flew back to the tree and replaced the Blue Dust. James grabbed the bottle and then threw Zarina into the water anyway.

The fairies rushed to rescue Zarina. They managed
to pull the lantern to the surface, but Zarina was still
in trouble because water was pouring into the lamp!

The fairies struggled with the latch. Finally, it opened just in time and the other fairies flew Zarina to the safety of the rocks to dry off.

Zarina was grateful to Tink and her friends.
She apologized and offered to help them catch James.
    Zarina led the fairies to the flying ship, but the second
star was not far away. They slipped into the captain's cabin
undetected – and reappeared looking like swashbucklers!
The real pirates couldn't believe their eyes.
    "Get them off my ship!" James commanded.

The fairies quickly realized their tiny weapons were useless against the pirates, so they used their talents instead! Fawn blasted a pirate with a sunbeam, knocking him overboard.

As Zarina fought James, she managed to trap him with the mast and snatch the Blue Dust from him.

Zarina spun the wheel of the ship and it began to tilt. James's precious golden dust streamed off the ship and when James reached for it, he fell.

As Zarina helped the other fairies, James, now covered in golden dust, flew up behind her and claimed the Blue Dust back.

But he dropped one speck. Zarina quickly grabbed it and threw it on James who then rocketed into the air, out of control. "From a trickle to a roar," she said with satisfaction.

Then, Tink used her water talent to create a giant wave in James's path, washing off all the golden dust. He crashed into the sea, where the crocodile swam after him.

The fairies had won! They took control of the ship and flew it back to Pixie Hollow. When they reached the amphitheatre, Zarina used her dust to wake the sleeping crowd.

"Zarina?" Fairy Gary exclaimed. "You're home!" And he pulled her into a giant hug.

"She even grew a Pixie Dust Tree!" exclaimed Rosetta. Now, they had two.

Queen Clarion was
so impressed that
she granted Zarina
permission to show off
her new talent.

Colours flew as Zarina
gave her friends back
their original talents and
the crowd was in awe!